RABBIT'S SNOW DANCE

✳ DANCE ✳

a traditional Iroquois story

As told by

JAMES & JOSEPH BRUCHAC

Illustrated by

JEFF NEWMAN

SCHOLASTIC INC.

For Ava Rae, the newest member of our storytelling family
—*J.B. & J.B.*

For Jodi —*J.N.*

ISBN 978-0-545-70606-3

Text copyright © 2012 by Joseph Bruchac and James Bruchac. Illustrations copyright © 2012 by Jeff Newman. All rights reserved.
Published by Scholastic Inc., 557 Broadway, New York, NY 10012, by arrangement with Dial Books for Young Readers,
an imprint of Penguin Young Readers Group, a division of Penguin Random House LLC. SCHOLASTIC and associated logos
are trademarks and/or registered trademarks of Scholastic Inc.

12 11 10 9 8 7 6 5 4 3 2 1   16 17 18 19 20 21

Printed in the U.S.A.   40

First Scholastic printing, November 2016

Designed by Jennifer Kelly
Text set in Mrs Eaves
The illustrations for this book are rendered in watercolor, gouache, and ink.

Long ago, they say, Rabbit did not look the
way rabbits do today. Back then Rabbit had a very
long, beautiful tail.

But even though his tail was long, his patience was
short. Whenever Rabbit wanted something, he would
chant, "I want it, I want it, I want it right now!"

One day Rabbit was wishing it would snow.

Why?

With feet so big that they were like snowshoes, Rabbit could hop right on top of the snow and reach much higher into the trees for tasty leaves and buds.

The only problem was that it was summertime, and as everyone knows, it is not supposed to snow in the summer.

Rabbit, though, was impatient. "I want snow," he said. "I want it, I want it, I want it right now!"

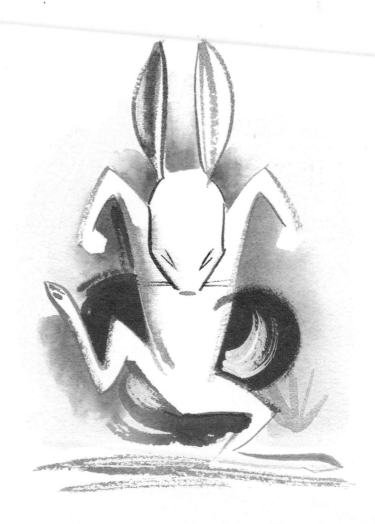

Rabbit knew a special song to make it snow. In the winter he would sing that song and dance in a circle playing his drum, and it would snow every time. He had never tried it in the summer because that was not the right season for a snow song. But Rabbit did not want to wait.

He ran through the forest to get his drum, chanting:

I will make it snow,
AZIKANAPO!
I will make it snow,
AZIKANAPO!

Azikanapo. That word means it will snow foot wrappers, great big flakes of snow.

So, when the other animals heard Rabbit singing, some of them got worried.

Chipmunk and Squirrel tried to stop him.

"It is too soon for snow," they said. "We haven't finished gathering enough nuts for the winter."

But Rabbit ran right past them and kept on chanting.

I will make it snow,
AZIKANAPO!
I will make it snow,
AZIKANAPO!

Beaver and Turtle looked up from their pond as Rabbit ran by.

"I haven't finished my dam," Beaver complained.

"I am not ready to go to sleep for the winter," Turtle said.

But Rabbit ran past them too, still chanting.

Other animals heard Rabbit, but did not believe him.

"That will never happen," Moose rumbled.

"Making it snow in the summer is almost as hard as stopping the sun from coming up," Bear growled.

Soon Rabbit reached his home. He took out his drum and began to sing his snow song as he danced in a circle.

"EE-OOO!"
Thump! Thump!
"EE-OOO!"
Thump! Thump!
"YO, YO, YO!
YO, YO, YO!"

Small flakes of snow began to fall from the sky. That made Rabbit happy. But there was not enough snow yet for him to reach the tender buds in the branches above him.

"A *little* snow is good," Rabbit said. "*More* snow is better."

"EE-OOO!"
Thump! Thump!
"EE-OOO!"
Thump! Thump!
"YO, YO, YO!
YO, YO, YO!"

All over the forest, animals saw the snow falling. The ones
with big wide feet, like Lynx and Otter and Grouse, were
pleased. They liked the snow and enjoyed playing in it. They
even sang along.

"EE-OOO!"
Thump! Thump!
"EE-OOO!"
Thump! Thump!
"YO, YO, YO!
YO, YO, YO!"

Other animals were not pleased. They were small, and
the deep snow was now over their heads.

Rabbit did not notice their troubles. He just kept on
singing.

"EE-OOO!"
Thump! Thump!
"EE-OOO!"
Thump! Thump!
"YO, YO, YO!
YO, YO, YO!"

Now the snow was so deep that it came up to the chests of the bigger animals. They all rushed for shelter.

Soon Rabbit was able to reach those tender buds on the trees. But he was not satisfied.

If *a lot* of snow is good, then a lot *more* snow will be better, he thought.

So he kept on singing. All of the animals had left to find shelter, but Rabbit was too foolish to stop. He just kept on singing and dancing and playing his drum.

When the snow had gotten so deep that it covered the tops
of all but one of the tallest trees, Rabbit realized he was tired.
He stopped singing.

"I think I need to take a nap," he said. He hopped into the
top of that one tall tree that still stuck out above the snow,
and fell asleep.

Rabbit slept all night. Even when dawn came, he kept on sleeping. Now the summer sun began to shine. All of that snow began to melt.

It melted down below the tops of the trees.

It melted down below the middle of the trees.

It melted down below
the bushes.

It melted down below
the grass.

Soon all of the snow was gone.

The other animals were happy. They came out again and began to do all the things animals do in the summer.

Rabbit, though, was still asleep high, high up in the top of the tallest tree. Finally, near the end of the day, he woke up.

"Time to hop around on all my snow," Rabbit said.

He had not yet wiped the sleep from his eyes. He didn't see that the snow was gone, so when he stepped from the top of that tree he got a big surprise.

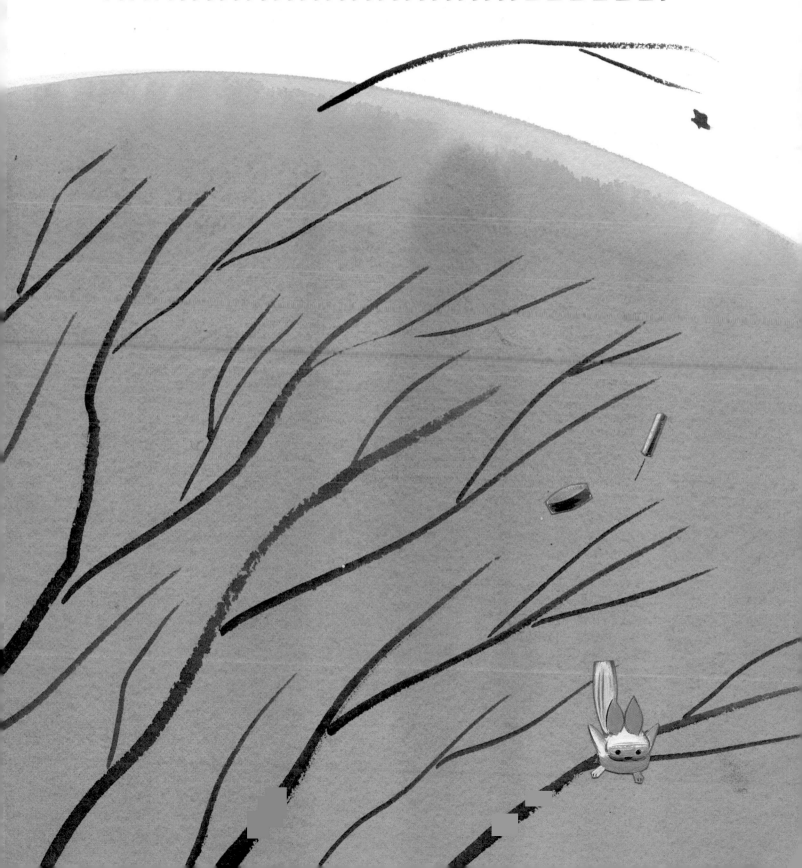

Rabbit fell, and as he fell, that long tail of his caught on one branch after another. Each time, a little bit was pulled off. Finally, *ka-boom!* Rabbit hit the ground.

His tail felt funny. He turned back to check it, and saw that almost all of that long tail was gone! He looked up. Pieces of his tail were stuck on the tips of the tree branches.

Ever since then, at the time of year when the snow goes away, you can see those little furry pieces of Rabbit's tail stuck on certain trees. Some call them pussy willows, but those who know about Rabbit's snow dance know what they really are.

To this day Rabbit has a short tail. And even though he still loves the snow, he has learned to be more patient. He no longer sings his snow song in the summertime.

However, during the colder months, if you keep an open ear toward the forest, you may just hear a small voice singing this song:

"EE-OOO!"
Thump! Thump!
"EE-OOO!"
Thump! Thump!
"YO, YO, YO!
YO, YO, YO!"

When you hear that, you'd better head for home.
Soon it will begin to snow.